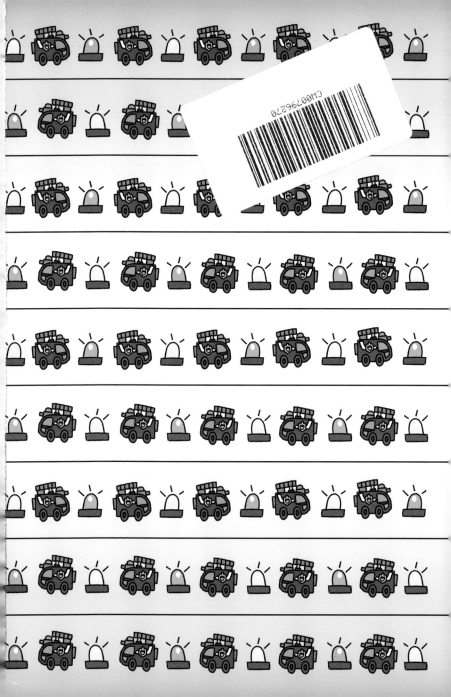

To Jen – for reading all my sister post! – T.C.
For Sam, who's my magical superhero – S.W.

(With special thanks to Perranporth Community
Fire Station, Freddie Martin and Remy Whiting)

Unicorns in Uniforms: Dragon Inferno is a uclanpublishing book

First published in Great Britain in 2025
by uclanpublishing
University of Central Lancashire
Preston, PR1 2HE, UK

Text copyright © Tracy Curran, 2025
Illustrations © Steve Wood, 2025
Photographs p108-111 © Shutterstock, Remy Whiting and
Perranporth Community Fire Station, 2025

978-1-916747-42-5

1 3 5 7 9 10 8 6 4 2

Set in 14/18.5pt Ysabeau Infant by Amy Cooper

A CIP catalogue record for this book is available from the British Library.
Printed and bound in Great Britain by Page Bros Ltd, Norwich

UNICORNS IN UNIFORMS

Dragon Inferno

UCLan Publishing

MEET THE UNICORNS

Blaze
Firefighter

Locke
Police Sergeant

Dash
Paramedic

Sunny
Air and Mountain
Rescue

Aquarius
Sea Rescue

MEET THE VEHICLES

Quench
The Flamequencher

Pat
The Patroller

Bee
The Unicopter

Bow
The Rainbowlance

UNICORN RAP!

The Unicorns in Uniforms would like to welcome you
to Sunshine Realm, their special home.
Come on and meet the crew!
These unicorns save creatures' lives –
they love the job they do.
But before we start the story,
let's discover WHO is WHO!

Well . . .

First, there's Blaze and Quench – they're the firefighting team.
Blaze is fair but fiery, and she likes to let off steam.
She's a very loyal protector, whereas Quench just likes to play.
I'd watch out for his mischief – if his hose is on, he'll SPRAY!

Then, there's Sergeant Locke who has a cool police car, Pat.
He's a snorer and a baker and he doesn't like to chat.
His heart is made of gold, although he's SUPER strict on rules.
Because Locke's the one in charge and he has no time for fools . . .

Sunny flies up high inside his unicopter, Bee.

They're the fastest on the scene in an emergency.

Sunny's super healthy with a funky rainbow mane,

while Bee is proud and queenly (oh and, yes, a little vain).

Dash, the paramedic – WAIT! – is NOT a unicorn.

She's a rare and special zebra and the one without a horn.

But everybody loves her, for with Bow, her Rainbowlance,

She'll race to care for others . . . and she really likes to dance.

Aquarius the narwhal is as playful as can be.

For a narwhal is a unicorn who lives beneath the sea.

She's dizzy and she's whizzy and she's super, duper fast.

But Whizzy isn't whizzy – he's a boat who's always last!

So now you've met the rescue crew, it's time to turn the page.

Blaze is needed urgently – a fire's begun to rage.

But can she keep her temper, like a rescue worker should?

And remain cool and collected as she heads . . .

into . . . the wood . . .

Sparks in the Sky

It had been a busy morning. Blaze's tummy grumbled loudly as she and her emergency vehicle, Quench, pulled up in front of the Unicorns in Uniforms' headquarters. The grumpy sound coming from her stomach matched Blaze's mood. She was soaking wet and muddy, all thanks to Quench's love of mischief.

"It's a *double* wash and polish for you," Blaze scolded the fire engine, turning

down her very loud music. She breathed in the calming view of Sizzling Sands beach, which stretched out in front of the headquarters, and pressed the button on her key ring that activated the doors to the headquarters garage. "Your hosepipe tricks are tickling my temper!"

A noise that sounded very much like a hiccup echoed through Quench's dashboard. Quench was a brilliant emergency vehicle, but he liked to have fun on the job. Already that morning, during a charity car wash, he'd turned his water jets on at full power and given everyone a soaking. Then, after dealing with a nasty kitchen fire at The Bakehorse Bakery, he'd managed to get Bagel, the bakery's dog, stuck on the roof by shooting him into the air on a fountain of water. He'd created so many muddy puddles, the bakery was now surrounded by ducks.

"Is that your idea of an apology?" tutted Blaze, as she drove Quench into his parking bay.

Quench blew a raspberry and Blaze's grumpy scowl broke into a smile. As annoying as her emergency vehicle was, there was no way she would be without him. She liked his spirit too much.

Blaze turned the radio back up to full volume, grabbed a bucket and sponge and scrubbed at Quench's flame red bodywork until it was spotless. The fire engine showed his disapproval at being cleaned by blasting his horn in time to the beat of the music, promptly giving Blaze a headache.

The pink-nosed unicorn ignored it and scrubbed twice as hard. Blaze could be fiery and impatient, but she loved her job and had super-high standards. By the time she had finished polishing, her bright pink mane and shiny golden horn, which swirled like sunshine, were gleaming with sweat. Blaze searched for any specks of dirt she might have missed, but there were none. She nodded in satisfaction.

"Now it's time to clean myself up," she told Quench, "and then I'm going to pop to the Mane Control Room before whipping up some spicy fajitas for lunch."

Blaze loved spicy food, even though the other unicorns joked that it inflamed her temper.

Blaze clip-clopped upstairs to the unicorns' living quarters and into the cluttered and messy dormitory she shared with Sunny, Locke and Dash. Hanging off her top bunk was a clean, blue firefighting uniform that had the Unicorns in Uniforms logo embroidered on the jacket pocket and yellow high-vis stripes sewn across the body. Blaze smiled. The Sunshine Realm, with its mishmash of fantasy creatures and animals, really was a beautiful place and she was proud to be one of the emergency workers who kept everyone happy, safe and protected.

Suddenly, the dormitory went dark. Blaze glanced up just in time to see a huge figure flash past the window.

"What was that?" She frowned. The Unicorns in Uniforms were trained to be on constant alert and that shadow had been too big to be any kind of seabird, even an albatross. Quickly, Blaze stuck her head out of the window.

"**GAH!**" A jet of hot flames shot down from the rooftop, scorching Blaze's mane and almost melting the tip of her horn.

Then came a giggle and the scrabbling of claws.

Red dots of fury danced in Blaze's eyes as she dashed into the bathroom, stuck her head in the sink and turned on the cold tap to extinguish any lingering sparks. After all the safety talks she'd given throughout the realm, someone was playing with fire on the roof of their emergency headquarters!

With her soaking wet mane dripping water in her eyes, Blaze raced outside and looked up. More giggling sounded from the rooftop of the cubed building, followed by a flash of silver.

"Who's there? Come down at once!" Blaze demanded.

There was a scuffle and then silence. Blaze huffed. She was going to have to get a ladder. Or . . . maybe Aquarius had seen who was messing about? She trotted towards the Mane Control Room.

The Mane Control Room was a big boathouse that was attached to the side of the main headquarters building. It had been cleverly designed so Aquarius, the sea-rescue narwhal – who was known as a *'unicorn of the sea'* – could swim inside from her rockpool, monitor the control panel and keep track of any emergency calls via a waterproof headset.

"Aquarius?" called Blaze, motioning for her to swim outside. "Did you just see . . . ?"

But Blaze didn't get to finish her sentence.

A bright trail of fire whooshed across the sky as *two* large, winged beasts, shadowy in the sun, launched themselves off the roof of the headquarters and dived

towards them at a frightening speed. Blaze whinnied in alarm. They were going way too fast to stop, and there was no time for her to do anything but . . .

The Fun Police

With a playful roar, a smattering of sparks and a huge rush of air, the shadows zoomed straight over Blaze's head, promptly knocking her into Aquarius' rockpool.

"**Agggh!**" The water was freezing! Thankfully, as she kicked out, Blaze could feel Aquarius pushing her back up to the surface.

Snorting in fury, Blaze struggled out of the pool and squinted into the sunlight. Swooping and somersaulting through the

sky were two young dragons from Dragon Desert. The firefighter recognised them instantly. Flare, with his green and blue scales and gold-tipped leathery wings, was the youngest son of the Kindling family – bold and boisterous and often in trouble. The other dragon was his friend, Glimmer. She was slightly smaller with purple, silver-flecked scales and a bright pink ridge down her back.

"Just what do you think you're doing?" shouted Blaze, sparks practically shooting out of her own nostrils as the dragons dive-bombed again. This time, their trail of flames singed the top of her ears.

"***Get down here this instant!***"

Flare let out a nervous giggle at Blaze's tone.

"We're only messing about!" he called.

"Yeah, we're just having a bit of fun!" echoed Glimmer.

"Fun?" Blaze snorted. "You'll set the whole realm on fire. I said get down here . . . **NOW!**"

The dragons' looked at each other and shrugged their wings before flying down to the side of the pool.

"Blaze," Aquarius's tinkly voice danced softly across the water, her long rainbow tooth shimmering in the light. "Go easy on them. They're only playing."

Blaze snorted. "I will *not* go easy, Aquarius," she hissed under her breath.

"Two careless young dragons on the loose is a recipe for disaster. You know that!" She turned to glare at the youngsters, who were watching her nervously. Their wings were pressed flat against their bodies and their tails drooped.

"**GO. HOME. THIS. INSTANT!**" she ordered, waving her hoof. "Before I call your parents."

Glimmer whimpered.

"We didn't mean any harm," sniffed Flare.

Blaze softened.

"That's all very well," she said, in a gentler tone. "But at your age, you haven't yet mastered full control of your fire-breathing. Just a few stray sparks could cause a lot of damage. Promise me you'll fly straight home, and we'll say no more about it."

Flare and Glimmer nodded miserably.

"Anyone would think she's the fun police, not the firefighter," grumbled Flare, as they rose into the air.

"Yeah," giggled Glimmer, blowing a raspberry. "**BORING!**"

Blaze turned as red as fire. Glimmer was just as cheeky as Quench, except when Quench blew raspberries he didn't release thousands of burning fireflies into the sky.

Blaze's eyes widened in horror as the sizzling sparks drifted dangerously close to the Mane Control Room. Thankfully, before they could settle, Aquarius shot a stream of water out of her blowhole and extinguished them.

"Those mischievous monsters didn't listen to a word I said," cried Blaze in outrage.

"OK, OK, keep your mane on, Blaze," joked Aquarius. "The only thing that's caught fire is your temper. Let's try some deep breaths and then count to ten, shall we?"

Blaze's muscles tensed. The other unicorns were always trying to get her to control her temper. Sunny kept booking her in to do yoga with the yetis and Dash kept buying her lavender bubble bath so she could take long bubbly soaks in their bathgroom. Blaze didn't have the time or patience for any of that, but she had to admit that Aquarius's breathing exercises did actually help. Staying calm and focussed was an important part of the job.

"I don't know, Aquarius," she said, as she breathed in the fresh salty sea air. "I have a really bad feeling about this."

Right at that moment, her uniphone started to vibrate and the Disturbance Detection Screen inside the boathouse began to bleep. Aquarius swam inside to check it.

"It's Sunny calling!" said Blaze, her heart filling with dread. Sunny and his alicopter, Bee, were the Unicorns in Uniforms' air and mountain rescue team and they spent most of their time patrolling the skies over The Sunshine Realm. Had they spotted Flare and Glimmer?

"Blaze?" Sunny's voice was shaky. "You need to get to Witchy Wood pronto. Two young dragons just flew out of nowhere and collided straight into us. They've fallen into the wood and . . . the trees have caught fire!"

The Race to Splintery Bridge

With Sunny still on the uniphone, Blaze left Aquarius dealing with calls in the Mane Control Room and galloped to Quench's parking bay as fast as her hooves could carry her. This was *exactly* the situation she'd been dreading.

"Can you do a water drop, Sunny?" she asked. Dropping a torrent of water from the air was the best way to deal with a woodland fire.

"I'm sorry, Blaze." Sunny's voice sounded sorrowful. "I've had to make an emergency landing. Those dragons crashed into us with some force and Bee's going to need a thorough examination before she's safe to fly again."

Blaze snorted in frustration but then remembered her breathing.

"OK, Sunny," she said. "I'll handle things. You stay safe and get Bee checked."

Blaze ended the call and jumped into Quench's driving cab. With his wheels screeching loudly, she drove him onto the road.

"Activate lights and siren!" she ordered, speaking into the fire engine's interactive

dashboard. "And switch on all of your sensors."

Quench gave a cheeky **poop-poop -de-do** with his horn and distorted his siren to sound like the quacking ducks that had swamped the bakery that morning. Blaze sighed impatiently.

"Come on, Quench!" she whinnied. "There's a time and a place for messing about and this is definitely NOT it. We have a serious, large-scale emergency on our hooves and I need you to *focus*!"

With a sheepish beep, Quench's siren changed to its normal high-pitched wail and the pair raced at maximum speed up the road that separated Dizzy City from Witchy Wood. Above the trees an orange glow was lighting up the sky. It was growing brighter and brighter by the second, and billows of black smoke belched upwards in spiralling towers. But there were other shapes too, swarming out of the trees. Blaze peered through Quench's windscreen, but she was too far away to see clearly. Were they bats?

"Activate your thermal radar," she told Quench. Quench beeped and immediately the screen on his dashboard lit up with a close-up image of the flying figures. Their outlines were clear, and they rippled with reds and oranges – the colour of warmth.

"They're witches and wizards. They're escaping the fire on brooms!" exclaimed Blaze. "And fairies, too!" She slammed her foot on Quench's accelerator pedal. "We need to hurry. The trees are dry, and those flames will spread fast. Not everyone may be able to escape." The Sunshine Realm had recently been enjoying a heatwave but, right now, Blaze would have welcomed some rain.

As they rounded a bend in the road, Blaze caught sight of Locke. The police unicorn was standing next to his police car, a speed camera and a lime green racing car. There had been some recent reports of vehicles driving too fast around the realm and it looked like Locke had caught one of the culprits. Sedgewick Spadefoot, a rich, mean toad who owned the Sunshine Savings bank, was standing next to Locke and, by the look on his face, he was furious at being pulled over. Blaze gritted her teeth.

"Uh oh, the last thing we need is any trouble from Sedgewick," she muttered to Quench. "That old windbag is full of hot air, and hot air and fire do **NOT** mix!"

She bit her lip as she thought of her own temper. Sedgewick wasn't the only one who was sometimes full of hot air. She shook the thought away and took another deep, calming breath.

The speed camera let off a huge flash as they sped past, but Blaze ignored it. This was an emergency! She turned Quench down a muddy track that led into Witchy Wood. Together, they swerved this way and that, thumping through potholes and dodging the thick branches that reached towards them with grasping fingers. Witchy Wood stretched down the whole east side of the realm but, unfortunately, it wasn't easy to access.

"Of all the places those dragons could have crash-landed," grumbled Blaze, "it had to be the woods. And it looks like the fire is on the other side of the river. We're going to have to cross it!"

The Roaring River ran right down the middle of the woods and posed a *big* problem. Quench flashed up a map on his screen and beeped loudly.

"You're right, Quench!" said Blaze, understanding what the fire engine was trying to say. Her emergency vehicle liked to use noises rather than speech to communicate and she was used to it by now. "Splintery Bridge is the best way to

get across the river. In fact, it's the *only* proper crossing at all. Let's head there."

Blaze veered left towards the bridge, monitoring their position on Quench's map. The smoke was growing thicker, and she could barely see through the windscreen anymore. Witches and wizards staggered out of the gloom. All of them were coughing and spluttering and protective spells were flying here, there and everywhere.

But it seemed their magic wasn't working well in the heat. One kind witch kept conjuring a bubble shield around a cluster of fairies, but it just kept popping.

"Where are your brooms?" Blaze shouted to them through the driver's window.

"We didn't have time to grab them," coughed an elderly witch. "The flames were so fierce, we barely got out ourselves."

Blaze nodded. As useful as brooms were, wasting time trying to find one was a huge no-no when there was a fire raging.

"You did the right thing," she said. "Keep moving, try not to panic and we'll get you out of here." She grabbed her uniphone to call Locke and Dash. She needed Locke to leave his speed camera and come and lead everyone to safety. Dash, the Unicorns in Uniforms' paramedic, could then perform checks on everyone. Smoke inhalation was incredibly dangerous and some creatures would need some extra oxygen.

But as Splintery Bridge loomed through the black smog, it was Blaze who had to stop herself from panicking. On the far side of the river, a terrifying monster of flames was racing towards the wooden crossing. Orange tongues of heat licked the first planks and the air hissed and crackled with anger. It was too late to drive across.

"There are creatures still trapped over there!" whinnied Blaze in alarm, as she activated Quench's thermal radar again. The screen showed a huddle of figures crouched on the opposite side of the riverbank.

"I don't think it's Flare and Glimmer," she said, trying to make out the shapes, "but whoever they are, they're in urgent need of rescuing. Then we'll have to find the dragons."

But with the first plank of the bridge now fully alight, the seriousness of the situation hit her with the force of one of Sergeant Locke's snores.

If the bridge fell and there was no other way across the water, this inferno was going to turn . . .

deadly.

The Battle
for the Bridge

There wasn't a moment to lose. If Blaze was going to rescue everyone who was trapped, including the missing dragons, she *had* to beat the flames back from the bridge. Holding her breath, she jumped down from the safety of Quench's driving cab and into the smoke. The toxic fumes immediately invaded her muzzle, choking her throat and lungs.

"Time for my breathing apparatus," Blaze told herself, as she fought her way blindly to Quench's rear end and threw open his back doors. The first and most important rule of being a firefighter was to always wear full protective gear.

Quickly, Blaze heaved a cylinder of air onto her back, which was attached to a breathing tube and mask. Then she jammed her custard yellow helmet back onto her head, which had a hole cut in the front for her horn, pulled on a thick pair of fireproof mittens and unravelled Quench's largest hose onto the bridge. Flames reared up in front of her and the wooden planks creaked and groaned under her hooves. Time was running out to save it.

"Activate foam, Quench!" she thought in her head, knowing that her emergency vehicle would already be on it. He was. With a whoosh and a hiss, the hosepipe swelled, and a torrent of foam gushed out.

Blaze aimed the hose at the inferno and blasted it with gallons of bubbly liquid.

The foam wasn't magical, but it was more effective than water – a potion that would save lives. Blaze sprayed and sprayed, extinguishing the flames on the bridge. The inferno roared furiously at her. It was too huge and hungry for her to overpower it, but she just needed to force it back long enough to save the lives of those trapped . . .

A blue flashing light behind her suddenly caught her attention. Locke had arrived in his police car, Pat. He parked next to Quench, scraping Pat's bumper on several tree trunks in the smog, and stumbled towards Blaze. His hooves were clamped over his muzzle.

Still holding the hose, Blaze backed up to let Locke speak. She didn't want anyone on the bridge that didn't need to be.

"I came as fast as I could," Locke spluttered to Blaze. With her breathing mask on, he sounded like a distant echo. "You deal with the fire, and I'll lead everyone out. Dash is waiting out on the road with Bow."

Blaze nodded, pointing to her mask and then to Quench.

"Breathing apparatus!" she mimed. Locke nodded to show he understood and went to get himself a mask and tank.

Blaze inched back onto the bridge and continued her battle with the flames. Finally, she managed to beat them back enough to step onto the far side of the riverbank. The bridge was charred and smouldering, but it was still standing . . . just!

"*Quick! Quick!*"

Blaze signalled to the huddle of shadows with one hoof as she tried to keep control of the hose with the other.

The shadows hobbled towards her, hunched and choking. As they got closer, Blaze made out two wizards holding the hands of a mini-wizard. Both of the adults had their wands out and were trying to conjure a bubble shield over the mini-wizard's head. But just like with the fairies, it kept popping. Blaze waved them onto the bridge.

But there was another shadow coming too. It was huge, wobbly and . . .

Blaze squinted through the smoke and whinnied in surprise.

A young witch, who she recognised immediately as Dash's friend, Jinx, was struggling towards her. She had a large, misshapen goldfish bowl over her head, which looked like the product of a spell gone wrong. She was pushing a very odd, wheeled contraption that was *definitely* the product of a spell gone wrong. It looked like a cross between an enormous wheelbarrow and a supermarket trolley. But whatever it *actually* was, Blaze didn't care. For lying inside it, with bashful yellow eyes, was . . .

Flare the dragon!

Jinx's Jinx

Blaze's heart soared with relief but . . . there was no sign of Glimmer.

"Oh thank – **cough** – goodness you're here," panted Jinx, as Blaze strained to hear what the witch was saying. "What an absolute – *cough* – drama this is! I was enjoying a stroll through the woods, when there was a humongous – *cough* – **CRASH**, a bright trail of light, and this – *cough* – fellow nearly landed on top of me." She pointed to Flare.

"The next minute, everything was on – *cough* – fire. By the way, have you seen my – *cough* – grandmother, Hex? She lives with me in the north of the wood. Thank goodness the fire isn't headed in – *cough* – *that* direction." She turned to tut at something over her shoulder. "Oh do, come on, Gonzales!"

From out of the gloom, a tortoise came plodding towards them. He was about the size of a dinner plate and the pattern on his shell was as swirly as the choking smoke. Blaze blinked in astonishment.

"You really – *cough* – are on the go-slow, today!" sighed Jinx.

Gonzales looked outraged. "I am ALWAYS on the go-slow!" he wheezed. "And considering the urgency of the situation we're in, a lift wouldn't go amiss."

Jinx rolled her eyes before scooping him up and plonking him on her shoulder.

Annoyance rose up in Blaze's chest. She was incredibly grateful that Jinx had saved Flare but this was hardly the time for a chitchat. Right now, she needed Jinx to follow the other wizard family and push Flare across the bridge as quickly as possible. Although . . . she wasn't sure the bridge would hold their weight.

Jinx, however, seemed completely oblivious to the fact they were in the middle of an inferno. Despite the intense heat, she was still wearing her patchwork cloak and a long, knitted rainbow scarf. Jinx liked to knit . . . a **LOT**! She also liked to perform spells **VERY** badly and was the granddaughter of Hex – the most brilliant witch in the Sunshine Realm. Sadly, Jinx had not been gifted any of her talent.

"The dragon seems to have a broken wing," she rambled on, "and as you're always saying that magic and medicine don't mix, I conjured up a . . . er . . . trolley instead. But speaking of magic, it looks like you might need my help here." She pulled her wand from the pocket of her cloak.

"I can turn the bridge into stone," she said. "Then it won't burn."

"**NooOo!**" Blaze tried to cry out but no sound was getting through her mask. Besides, it was too late. Jinx swished her wand . . . and cast a spell.

The middle of the bridge collapsed into the river, taking the two wizards and the mini-wizard with it. The hosepipe was wrenched out of Blaze's hooves and angry sizzles of steam rose up as smouldering wood sank into cold water.

Blaze whinnied in horror. With the bridge gone, the fire couldn't get across the river, but now there were three wizards, wearing heavy cloaks, battling to stay afloat in the water. Blaze watched helplessly. With herself, Jinx, Flare and Gonzales trapped on the burning riverbank, there was no way back to Quench and the hosepipe was also in the river.

There was only one thing for it.

Blaze ripped off her breathing apparatus and whinnied across to the other riverbank.

"Locke, are you there? Get the rescue boat and rope!"

No answer. Blaze looked desperately at the figures thrashing around in the river. She could hardly see them through the smoke and now the flames were surging forwards again, scorching her back. She faced

an impossible choice – if she dived into the water to save the wizards, what would she do with Jinx and Flare?

Then, just as all her hope was fading, across the water, through the smog, Locke appeared. He was dragging a yellow, inflatable boat, with oars clipped on the side of it. The rescue boat! With all his might, Locke launched it into the middle of the river.

"**Jump!**" he boomed.

A Spinny Situation

Blaze didn't need to be told twice. Pulling her breathing apparatus back on, she heaved Flare out of Jinx's contraption and launched him towards the boat. **Oof!** Half-flying and half-falling, he landed awkwardly, and the boat almost tipped.

Jinx was next. Blaze hooked one hoof around the witch's waist and leapt into the air. But she'd forgotten about Jinx's tortoise. Gonzales promptly flew off

Jinx's shoulder. His head and legs curled into his shell as he did a triple somersault and landed smack in the middle of the boat. With a squishy thump, Blaze and Jinx landed next to him.

"That's the fastest I've ever seen you move!" Jinx said to her tortoise. Gonzales poked his head out of his shell, his eyes burning indignantly.

Blaze reached out as Locke tossed her a bag full of rope. She chose the longest, thickest one and cast one end of it into the water. One of the wizards, who had the mini-wizard tucked under his arm, grabbed on tight and Blaze hauled them in. They flopped into the boat, gasping for breath. The mini-wizard started crying with shock.

The second wizard was further away and trickier to reach. Blaze used the oars to paddle towards him, but the river current was pulling the wizard downstream.

"Ooh, maybe I can help," said Jinx, as she raised her wand. "I can change the direction of the current!"

"**NO!**" Blaze leapt forwards, but her equipment was heavy. She was a fraction too late to stop the witch casting another spell . . . **WHOOSH!**

The water around the second wizard turned into a gigantic whirlpool!

"Jinx, what have you done?" Blaze screamed soundlessly into her mask as the wizard started spinning around the swirling hole. She threw the rope towards him but the force of the whirlpool ripped it out of her hooves.

The wizard in the boat pulled out his wand and tried to undo Jinx's spell. It didn't work.

"My wand's too wet – it's ruined!" he croaked.

There was no time to think. The wizard in the water was zooming round and round, faster and faster, and now the boat was being sucked towards the whirlpool too.

Blaze threw down her oars and lunged as far as she could over the side of the boat, into the mouth of the spinning water. She stretched out her front legs to try and reach the wizard but it was no use. The boat teetered and wobbled before starting to spin around the whirlpool's edge too. Blaze gasped. Any second now, she was going to topple overboard.

Suddenly, someone in the boat grabbed

her back legs, steadying her enough so she could reach further. The wizard was just below her but spinning much faster, a look of pure panic in his eyes. Blaze forced herself to breathe. *She* couldn't panic – everyone was depending on her.

Blaze waited . . . then darted as the wizard whizzed past. Her hoof hooked onto his cloak. She had him! With burning muscles, she hauled him up towards her and into the boat.

Phew! The wizard instantly collapsed with exhaustion, but there was no time for Blaze to rest. Grabbing the oars, she heaved on them with all her might.

"**Aggghh!**" Panic seized the unicorn as the boat tipped further towards the whirlpool's vortex. She forced the feeling away and gulped a deep breath of oxygen from her tank.

"You can do this!" she told herself firmly, determination echoing around her head. She pulled on the oars again . . . and again . . . and again. There was no way she was giving up until she'd rowed everyone away from danger. Fiery pain raged through her body as she heaved and hauled and heaved

and hauled until, finally, the whirlpool loosened its grip on them. They were in safer waters.

Blaze paddled as quickly as she could towards Quench, Pat and Locke.

One by one, Locke hauled them out of the boat and soon everyone was on dry land.

"Flare and the wizards need to go to Hope Hospital," she told Locke, as she checked everyone over. Flare's wing did look broken, and the wizards were cold and in shock.

"I'll get Dash to come and collect them," nodded Locke, reaching for his uniphone.

"And I HAVE to tackle this fire and find Glimmer, Jinx's grandmother and anyone else who may be trapped," said Blaze, pointing at the flames. The inferno seemed determined to try and cross the river and was now travelling up the highest tree branches which arched over the water. It wouldn't take long for the sparks to jump across to the trees on their side.

"Ooh! Maybe I can help," said Jinx, as she jumped to her feet, pointed her wand towards the branches . . .

and cast yet another spell.

7

The Crossing

WHOOSH!

A magical wind blew up, changing the direction of the flames. Within seconds, the inferno started raging northwards, up the far side of the riverbank.

"I really need to eat that wand," muttered Gonzales.

Red dots of frustration danced in front of Blaze's eyes.

"JINX!" she yelled, her temper getting the better of her. "Please stop interfering!"

"Wind and fire do **NOT** mix!" cried Locke.

"Oops!" whispered Jinx. "I was only trying to help." Her face turned pale and she twisted the edge of her cloak in fear. "Instead, I think I've just sent the fire in the direction of my treehouse. My grandmother *must* be there. She'd never leave her potions."

Blaze and Locke watched hopefully as the wizards got out their soggy wands to try and reverse Jinx's spell. But it really was no use. Their wands were totally ruined. Jinx's bottom lip trembled.

"Oh dear," she whimpered. "You have to save my grandmother, Blaze. She may be a brilliant witch but she's stubborn – her potions mean everything to her." She shifted nervously. "And I really should tell you that these potions are . . . er . . . highly magical. If they catch fire, there'll be a whole hocus-pocus of trouble."

Blaze's jaw dropped. "Your treehouse is full of extra-magical potions?" she gasped. "If the fire reaches them, who knows what could happen. They could blow up your treehouse, the woods . . . even the whole of the realm."

"And with this wind, you barely have any time," boomed Locke. "Jinx, I have a good mind to arrest you for interfering with the emergency services."

"It's a good job I carry my house on my back," muttered Gonzales. "Nothing to worry about then."

Jinx's eyes filled with tears, and Blaze felt a rush of sympathy for her. This whole situation was a disaster but it wasn't Jinx's fault. Even Flare and Glimmer hadn't realised the danger in what they were doing. Now it was up to her to sort things out and, just like Gonzales the tortoise, Blaze had the one thing she needed with her . . . Quench!

Leaving Locke and Dash to manage the patients, Blaze cantered to her emergency vehicle, reeled the hosepipe out of the river and jumped into the driver's seat.

"It's all down to us now, buddy," she said to the fire engine. "Let's chase the fire and find somewhere to cross the river."

BUMP.
THUMP. WHACK.
THWACK.

Quench roared to life. With his siren wailing and his lights flashing at double speed, they drove northwards up the riverbank.

Branches battered the sides of the fire engine, while others smacked the windscreen. It was a slow and frustrating obstacle course of tree trunks.

On the opposite side of the water, the fire was ahead of them. Blaze pressed harder on Quench's accelerator. Ideally, they needed to get ahead of the inferno before they found a place to cross. But, with Jinx's magical wind fanning the flames, that wasn't going to happen.

"We need to cross now!" decided Blaze, turning Quench to face the river.

But the riverbank was too high, and the water was too deep for the fire engine to cross. Quench flashed up a map of the river on his dashboard but nowhere looked safe enough. Upstream, the river got even wider.

Blaze looked uncertainly at two smoking tree trunks up ahead that had fallen across the water. Could Quench possibly drive across them? It would be incredibly risky and dangerous . . .

"We don't have a choice!" she whinnied.

Quench, however, had other ideas. With a roar of his engine, he flashed an instruction across his screen.

REVERSE. REVERSE.

Blaze snorted with impatience.

"Quench, what do you mean *reverse?* We need to go forwards not backwards. Unless . . . you don't mean . . . I hope you're not thinking what I *think* you're thinking?

Quench sounded his horn excitedly.

"You want to *jump* across?" cried Blaze. "Impossible!"

Quench blew a raspberry and flashed up a technical diagram on his dashboard

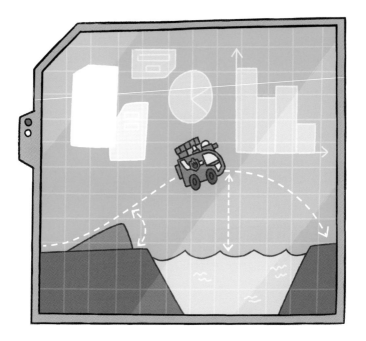

which showed some complex mathematical calculations to do with height and weight and speed. It seemed to prove that his idea was . . . er . . . unlikely . . . but *not* impossible.

Blaze gazed across the river, assessing the situation as quickly as she could. If Quench had any chance of jumping across, didn't he need some kind of ramp? But then . . . the riverbank on their side was steep, much higher than the opposite side. Maybe the extra height would be enough and . . . what other option did they have?

"You're right, Quench!" She grinned. "Nothing is impossible for **Unicorns in Uniforms**. Let's do it!"

Blaze reversed Quench as far back from the riverbank as she could. Then she revved the engine and floored the accelerator. Quench lurched forwards, rumbling towards the river at top speed, building up momentum. Blaze sensed her emergency vehicle's excitement as his wailing siren turned into a whoop. Then the ground fell away, and they launched into the air.

Over the river they sailed, the water rushing below them. Blaze gripped the steering wheel and hoped to goodness they'd make it to the other side. Quench was losing power and height now and they were only halfway across. Quench's wheels touched down amongst the flames

on the opposite riverbank. They'd **JUST** made it! But there was no way the fire engine could go any further. The trees on this side were packed too tightly together.

"Awesome work, Quench!" whinnied Blaze. "Now, activate the hose and I'll take it from here." She looked nervously at the inferno that was raging around them. It was the fiercest fire she had ever seen . . .

She had to call Sunny. Blaze grabbed her uniphone.

"Sunny, did you call a mechanic?" she coughed. "I need you and Bee back in the air. This fire is too big for me to deal with alone and there's a powerful wind making it worse. I need that water drop."

Sunny's cheerful voice sounded through the receiver loud and clear. "It's OK, Blaze. Bee's been checked and we're on it. We're flying northwards now."

Sighing with relief, Blaze checked her breathing apparatus, making sure she had a fresh tank of air. Then she rolled out Quench's hose. She needed to reach Jinx's treehouse

before the fire did. But, with the smoke blocking her view, she wasn't quite sure where the treehouse was . . .

Blaze attacked the inferno fiercely, blasting foam like she had never blasted foam before. The fire hissed and spat at her in fury, but Blaze's determination was fiercer. She sprayed and squirted and splattered and soaked every crackling flame – left and right, up and down – until, with a smoking sigh, they dissolved into spirals of steam and let her pass through to the next wave of burning trees.

Suddenly, Blaze caught sight of something shimmering up ahead, like an enormous shiny pearl. She squinted.

Was that a bubble shield?

It was! It was! And it was protecting something, just like Gonzales's shell protected him. It flared out around an aging oak tree like a puffy skirt and inside it was . . .

Jinx's treehouse.

"Found it!" thought Blaze triumphantly. "And that's the best bubble shield I've seen all day. Jinx's grandmother must be really powerful."

But Blaze had spoken too soon.

The inferno had surrounded the bubble shield and the spell was weakening under the heat. It wobbled and quivered like jelly until . . .

The bubble shield burst

and disappeared.

Cough
Catastrophe

As the fire leapt hungrily towards the treehouse, Blaze drenched the flames with foam. Her muscles were aching now, and her temper flared. Neither the fire nor the wind was giving in and if Hex's potions caught alight, then who knew what was going to happen?

Blaze took a deep calming breath and began to count. "**One ... two ... three ...**"

Immediately she felt her mind refocus. She could do this. She *had* to do this. She battled with all her might, beating the inferno back inch by inch . . .

One . . . Two . . . Three . . .

Suddenly, **WHOOSH!**

A torrent of water fell from the sky, drenching both herself and the fire. With a puff, the flames vanished, leaving just a few burning embers.

"Thank you, Sunny!" Blaze whooped into her mask. She didn't have to do everything by herself. One of the best things about being a Unicorn in Uniform was being part of a team.

Extinguishing the final few sparks, Blaze rushed towards the base of the oak tree. An old woman in a maroon cloak was bent over a purple, crumpled mound with silver flecks . . .

Glimmer!

"She's had a nasty bump to the head," croaked the woman, who was clearly Jinx's grandmother, "but I think she'll be OK. You got to us just in time!"

Blaze collapsed against the tree trunk. She was thirsty and exhausted, but Glimmer, Hex and the treehouse were safe! Slowly, she helped Glimmer sit up.

"I want my mum," whimpered the dragon. But as she spoke, she inhaled a swirl of smoke and began to cough.

And as she coughed, sparks flew out of her snout . . .

and sailed on Jinx's magical wind . . .

up to the treehouse.

Blaze turned to grab the hose, but it was too late. The treehouse burst into flames.

"My potions!" cried Hex, as she tried to scramble up the ladder.

Blaze grabbed hold of the witch and flung her over her shoulder in a firefighter's lift. Then she heaved Glimmer to her feet. If Hex's potions were as powerful as Jinx said they were, the treehouse might be about to blow. There was nothing to do but run.

But Glimmer was weak, and they were going too slow. A sinister silence thundered in Blaze's ears.

Three . . .

two . . .

one . . .

A loud bang rocked the woods. Glimmer wailed in terror.

"My potions!" cried Hex, again.

Blaze braced herself. Were they about to be blown off their feet or knocked unconscious? Had she failed to protect the Sunshine Realm?

But . . .

nothing happened. There was no fireball, no darkness – just the sizzling smell of candles on a birthday cake and a strange cacophony of whizzes and whistles, shrieks and squeals.

Blaze turned to look behind her and gasped.

Trails of colourful light were fizzing upwards: blues, golds, oranges and purples. They shimmered like glitterflies and sparkled like fireflies as they arced across the darkening sky. Then, with crackles and snaps and hisses and pops,

they burst into the most dazzling firework display the realm had ever seen.

Blaze gaped in awe as the colours danced across the sky. There had been no explosion and their home was no longer in danger.

"Your potions are EPIC!" she called to Jinx's grandmother, as she pulled off her breathing apparatus.

And Jinx's grandmother grinned.

And Breathe!

"Well, all's well that ends well," cried Aquarius, as she did a triple front somersault and squirted Blaze in the face with sea water. "You and Quench are quite the heroes, Blaze."

Blaze grunted. It was late evening and the Unicorns in Uniforms had gathered around Aquarius's rockpool for a debrief and supper. Glimmer and Hex had been taken to hospital and, after spending hours

trying to get Quench off the riverbank, he had had a *triple* wash and polish.

"We were only doing our jobs," she muttered as she took a huge bite of extra-spicy fajita. "Besides, we just got lucky with those fireworks so there's no need to make a fuss."

"Now, Blaze," boomed Locke, as he drained his cup of extra-strong coffee. "There's every need to make a fuss. You and Quench faced incredible danger with awesome bravery and lives were saved. That makes you a hero in my book!"

"You're a loyal, fierce and brilliant protector," said Dash, as she patted Blaze on the shoulder. "The Sunshine Realm is lucky to have you!"

Blaze flashed Dash a quick smile. The truth was, she was the lucky one. Being a Unicorn in Uniform and protecting the creatures of the realm meant everything to her.

"I really hope those dragons and Jinx have learnt their lesson," she said, refusing to sweeten her mood too much.

"Relax, Blaze!" said Sunny, who was stretching himself into a downward dog yoga pose. "Breathe in, deep and slow, just like the yeti's taught you."

Blaze snorted.

"Everything *is* fine, really." Dash nodded reassuringly at Blaze's frown. "The whole realm is pulling together. Everyone is making room in their homes for those who have been left homeless by the fire and it won't be long before they all have brand new treehouses and a LOT of new bridges. The gnomes and fairies have planted new tree saplings in the woods and are using their growing magic on them. Plus, Flare and Glimmer are recovering in hospital. Flare had a broken wing and Glimmer took a nasty knock to the head, but they're going to be OK."

"I don't think those two scallywags will be flying for a while, though," chuckled Locke. "Mama Kindling is furious with them. Not that they care. I hear they're creating merry mayhem up on the Infant Infirmary Ward. The nurses' temperatures have shot up!"

"Jinx offered to cast a calming spell on them when she paid them a visit," laughed Sunny. Both Jinx and her grandmother were staying in Hope Hospital overnight to be monitored for smoke inhalation.

"Jinx needs to stick to knitting from now on," said Blaze, folding her hooves, "or at least slow down and *think* before she casts spells. She should take a leaf out of her tortoise's book. If she doesn't, I'll feed her wand to Gonzales myself."

"I might take the nurses some of

my lavender bath brews," piped up Dash, ignoring Blaze's bad mood. "They really are very calming."

"I'm sure Blaze would like one too," Aquarius added cheekily. "It's been quite a long day."

Blaze shot Aquarius a withering look.

"Oh, go on, Blaze," pleaded Dash. "I'll even light some candles. You have to admit that staying calm really helped you today."

Blaze took a deep breath. She was struggling to stay calm now. Yoga and baths really weren't her thing. But, as she looked round at the other unicorns, she realised how much they cared about her and how much she loved them. They weren't just her teammates, they were her friends, and they only had her best interests at heart.

"Oh, go on, then," she muttered. "A yoga session and a lavender bubble bath sounds . . . er . . . relaxing. But I think I'll pass on the candles . . . I've seen enough flames for one day."

What's Inside a Fire Engine?

Blaze and Quench worked super hard to save everyone from Witchy Wood. But what do firefighters use in a real life emergency? Let's take a look inside an actual fire engine.

HOSE:

Blaze used an enormous hose to battle the dragon's inferno and so do our firefighters. A 'branch' goes on the end of the hose to control the water flow. But where does all the water come from? Firefighters use a 'hydrant key and bar' to access water from a hydrant or a water pipe in the road.

BREATHING APPARATUS:

It's very important that firefighters wear breathing apparatus, like Blaze, to protect themselves from smoke. A fire engine can have four sets of breathing apparatus inside it.

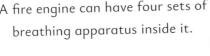

A RESCUE BOAT:

Blaze used an inflatable rescue boat to save the wizards from the river. Firefighters use these when there's not enough water for a real boat. Sometimes they are called 'inflatable rescue paths' or 'mud mats'. What would you call them?

A FIRST AID KIT:

Firefighters use first aid kits to help patients until an ambulance arrives. They also have defibrillators to help restart a patient's heart.

TORCHES:

Torches are essential to see in the dark.

RADIOS:

Blaze and the unicorns use uniphones to communicate but firefighters use radios. Radios allow firefighters to pass on important information and help them to work as a team.

THERMAL IMAGING CAMERAS:

Blaze and Quench use thermal imaging cameras in their rescue mission. Thermal imaging cameras detect heat, including body heat. This means firefighters can use them to track fires or find someone who is lost or trapped.

QUIZ

Can you remember what happened in the story?
Take this fun quiz to test your knowledge.

1. Where in The Sunshine Realm do the dragons, Flare and Glimmer, crash land?

a) Dragon Desert
b) Witchy Wood
c) Sizzling Sands Beach

2. What equipment does Blaze put on when she arrives at the scene of the fire?

a) A high-vis jacket and boots
b) A big thick cloak and scarf
c) Breathing apparatus and gloves

3. What is the name of Jinx's pet tortoise?

a) Gonzales
b) Slow-coach
c) Shelly

4. Jinx casts three disastrous spells. What happens on the FINAL spell?

a) She brews up a magical wind which changes the direction of the fire
b) The flames turn cold
c) Blaze falls into the water

5. Where does Jinx live with her grandmother, Hex?

a) In an underground cave
b) In a treehouse
c) In a house under Splintery Bridge

6. What happens when Hex's potions catch fire?

a) They cause a big explosion
b) They create a lightning storm
c) They turn into a huge firework display

7. What does Blaze NOT enjoy doing in his spare time?

a) Listening to loud music
b) Cleaning and polishing Quench
c) Doing yoga and taking bubble baths

IF YOU LIKED THIS, YOU'LL LOVE:

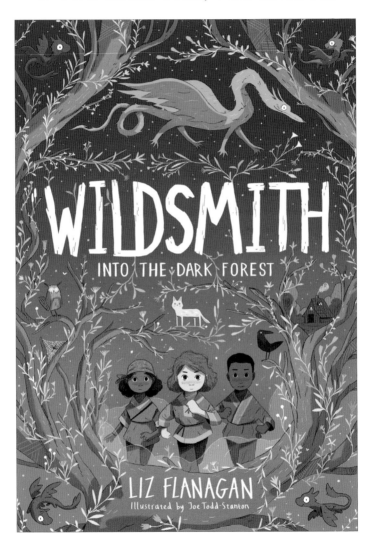

WILDSMITH

INTO THE DARK FOREST

LIZ FLANAGAN

Illustrated by Joe Todd-Stanton

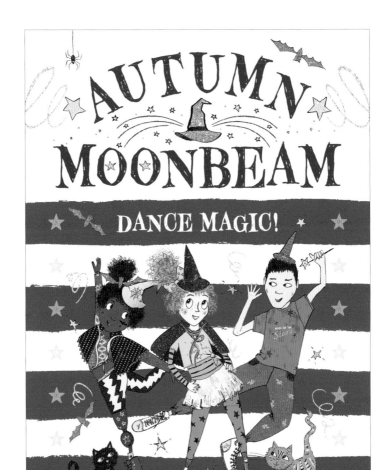

AUTUMN MOONBEAM

DANCE MAGIC!

EMMA FINLAYSON-PALMER & HEIDI CANNON

ESI MERLEH

MAGIC FACES

With colour
pictures by
**ABEEHA
TARIQ**

HEROES of the PIRATE SHIP

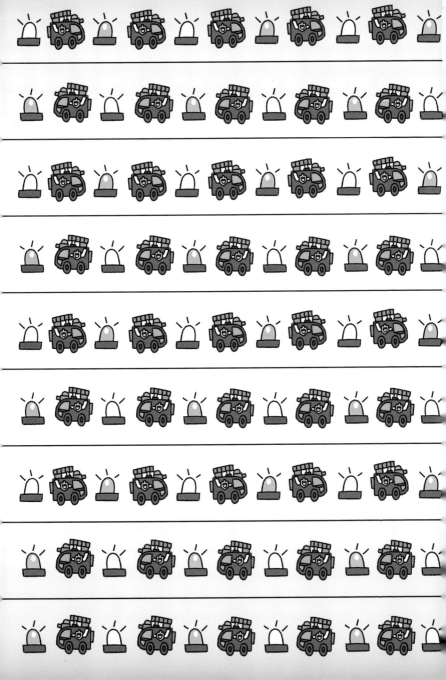